MW01033513

The Secret Cellar

a Dubois Files mystery

by Joan H. Young

cover illustration by Linda J. Sandow
interior illustrations by Joan H. Young

To Rex —
Joan H. Young

Published by Books Leaving Footprints
861 W US 10
Scottville, Michigan 49454

LCCN: 2018903678

ISBN: 0-9908172-6-1

ISBN-13: 978-0-9908172-6-0

DUBOIS FILES BOOKS

1. The Secret Cellar
2. The Hitchhiker
3. The ABZ Affair
4. The Bigg Boss

DEDICATION

To Carolyn Keene and
Franklin W. Dixon,
the collective identities of the authors
who have given young readers almost
a century of mysterious Nancy Drew and
Hardy Boys adventures.

CORA INTRODUCES HERSELF

My name is Cora Caulfield, and I'm an older lady now. But when I was a child, my last name was Dubois. That's French, pronounced dew-BWAH. I lived on the east side of the Thorpe River in Forest County, near where the Thorpe flows into the Petit Sable River. The year I turned nine, in early 1953, Jimmie Mosher moved into the house his grandfather had built on the west side of the Thorpe.

We became friends immediately. He was in the same grade at school, we rode the same bus, and we liked to do a lot of the same things. Things like exploring and trying new activities—if there was a puzzle to be solved, we were an unbeatable team. Friends who lived nearby sometimes joined our adventures.

I've been looking back on those years, and writing down our stories of the many mysterious happenings so they won't be forgotten. I hope you'll enjoy them.

Our first big success at solving a mystery was just after school let out for the summer that year. Jimmie's family had a big problem!

BOOK ONE - THE SECRET CELLAR

The East South River Road Neighborhood

1. Mosher
2. Szep
3. Dubois
4. Harris
5. Canning Factory
6. School
7. Store
8. R.R. Station

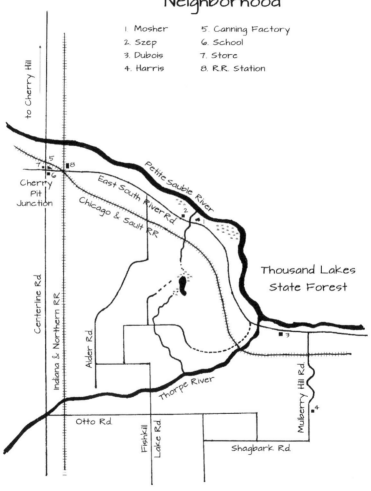

1. JIMMIE AND LASZLO

Jimmie Mosher frowned as he pushed his bicycle slowly through the dirt. He was on Mulberry Hill, more than four miles from home, on the far side of the Thorpe River. A few minutes ago he'd ridden over a sharp rock. The back tire popped and hissed. It went completely flat in two seconds. It was going to be a long hot walk home in the June sunshine. With his fair skin, he'd probably end up with a sunburn.

He kicked at another rock in disgust. This one didn't budge, and all Jimmie did was bruise his toe and drop the bike. "Ouch," he yelled, although there was no one nearby to hear him.

Yanking the bike upright from the dusty ground he continued shouting aloud, "Great. Summer vacation just started and now my tire is ruined. Where am I going to get the money for a new one?"

Behind him, a vehicle approached coughing

and banging loudly. He turned to see his neighbor's rusty and battered truck bouncing toward him with a brown dust cloud billowing around it. The truck stopped with squealing brakes beside the boy who sneezed as the dust swirled and settled.

"Put bike in back, Jimmie-boy. Hody vagy?"[1] Mr. Szep called cheerfully. "Laszlo, help."

From the bed of the pickup, Laszlo jumped to the ground. The neighbor's son was younger than Jimmie, and small. But he was stocky and strong. His short brown hair bristled from his head. Together the boys hauled the broken bicycle into the open truck. They grinned at each other and sat down with their backs against the cab.

Laszlo banged on the metal. "All set, Apa," he called, and the truck started moving.

Jimmie punched his friend on the arm. "Did your dad just call me a hedgehog?"

With a laugh, Laszlo answered. "It means 'how are you?'"

"That's goofy. What are you doing this

---

[1] say HODGE VODGE. How are you? in Hungarian.

2

summer?" Jimmie asked.

"Working on the farm. We have to pay the rent every month. It goes to your dad since your grandfather died."

"But why do you have to work? Don't your parents make enough money?"

"We all have to help. Apa and Anya[2] want to have enough so we can buy our own farm in a couple of years," Laszlo said.

"Yeah, but if you buy your own farm, you'll move away," Jimmie replied in a glum tone. "Maybe your mother and sisters shouldn't work so hard."

"We don't mind. Anya and my big sister Margit make pies and jam to sell. I'm raising chickens this year. Even baby Eniko is old enough that she can help pull weeds in the garden. We worked much harder when we lived in Hungary, and life was not so good there. I remember only a little. Apa says the government was very bad, and we had to leave. I'm glad we did."

"Me, too," Jimmie agreed.

---

[2] Apa and Anya. Father and Mother in Hungarian.

The boys stopped talking. It was difficult to be heard over the rattling and squeaking of the old truck.

"Hey, Mr. Szep," Jimmie yelled when the truck turned left at East South River Road. He turned around and banged on the back window of the cab. "The bridge is closed for repairs. I rode my bike over it okay, but you'll have to drive the truck around the long way."

"Not to worry, boys." The truck didn't slow down even a little bit.

"What's he going to do?" Jimmie asked his friend. "They put big stones for barricades, and the truck won't fit around them."

Laszlo laughed. "You'll see. Apa has a private road."

2. A NARROW ESCAPE

What are you talking about?" Jimmie demanded. "There aren't any other roads across the river here. I've lived here longer than you have. I should know."

"Not that much longer. Not in your grandfather's house, anyway."

"Yeah, but we visited lots, even when we lived in Shagway," Jimmie insisted. "I've been coming here since forever... before I can remember."

The truck reached the closed bridge. Large rocks had been placed by the county workers to keep drivers from crossing. Jimmie knew what he was talking about. There was absolutely no way a vehicle could work its way around that barrier. But Mr. Szep only slowed down a little bit as he turned left and drove south along the river. There wasn't any road there at all, only some faint ruts that might lead to a farmer's field.

They reached the railroad tracks and Mr. Szep put on the brakes.

"Hang on," Laszlo said, as he grabbed tightly to a bit of rope that was knotted through a ring in the truck's frame. He pointed to another cord on Jimmie's side.

"The tracks aren't that rough," Jimmie protested.

Laszlo laughed. "They will be in a minute."

The truck began to crunch across the large ballast rocks and then the wooden ties. When a front tire bumped over the first rail, Jimmie felt the truck turning. Mr. Szep was going to drive on the tracks and cross the river on the railroad bridge!

It wasn't scary at first. The truck fit pretty well with the left tires next to the left rail, and the right tires outside of the right rail, but when the bank of the river was behind them there was nothing but the ends of the ties and water visible below.

Jimmie tried to kneel and look over the side of the truck, but every time the tires thumped over a wide crack between the railroad ties it bounced his knees on the hard floor. That hurt. Looking down at the water moving sideways beneath him while the truck moved slowly forward made him feel sort of dizzy too. He sat back down and held tightly to his piece of rope.

They were halfway across when a train whistle sounded!

Jimmie and Laszlo looked at each other in fear.

"What was your dad thinking?" Jimmie whispered. At least he tried to whisper, but he might have been almost yelling to be heard above the noise of the truck as Mr. Szep sped up.

The bouncing increased, and neither boy was able to say anything at all. Jimmie felt as if his teeth were going to rattle out of his head. He clenched his jaws tight and held on.

Laszlo raised an arm and pointed to the rear, the way they were facing. Black smoke rose above the tree line and in another second, the round face of a huge steam engine came into view.

The river below them was forgotten. The boys

watched the coal car and two boxcars appear behind the engine as it came around a bend. The truck was bouncing so hard they lay down with heads cradled on their arms and their feet braced against the cab. The damaged bicycle bounced too and kept jabbing the boys in the ribs and legs. Jimmie wanted to hide his eyes, but he couldn't stop watching as the train came nearer and nearer. Its whistle shrieked again and the brakes began to squeal and spark on the metal rails.

Just then the truck lurched violently as it left the railroad tracks and entered a grassy pasture, coming to a stop.

The boys watched as if in a trance. The engine flew past them in a blur with the whistle blasting. This was very much closer than either of them had ever been to a moving train.

Jimmie glanced behind him into the cab of the truck. Mr. Szep was smiling and waving at the train as if nothing unusual had happened.

3. THE TENANT FARM

"A little adventure, eh *pacik*?[3] Maybe not to tell your *anyak*.[4]   The women like not so much," Laszlo's father joked. But he looked quite serious.

Now that the bridge was safely crossed, Laszlo and Jimmie were feeling strangely thrilled at having such a wild story to tell, but they agreed their mothers might not want to hear it.

With no further excitement, they reached the road on the west side of the river and drove slowly to the Szep's house. The Hungarian family lived next door to Jimmie. However, farm neighbors need more space than city neighbors. The two houses were almost an eighth-mile apart, about a two-minute walk.

Jimmie's father, Jed Mosher, owned both houses and all the surrounding land. The Szeps

---

[3]say PEE-sik. A pet name that means little horses.

[4]say ON-yak. Plural of anya. Mothers.

were tenant farmers. They paid their rent by working on the Mosher farm and also by giving Mr. Mosher some of the crops they grew on the rented land. Many families who came to the United States with very little money chose this arrangement in order to have a place to live while they tried to save enough to buy land of their own.

The Moshers weren't rich even though they owned two houses. Jimmie's grandfather, Jedediah, Senior, had built them both when he was young. He was a hard-working farmer who appreciated the help a tenant could provide. His wife, Maybella, liked having another woman nearby to work and visit with.

This past fall the older Jedediah had died. Jed, Junior and his wife, Hazel, with their son Jimmie, had moved into the house with Maybella in January. Jimmie had to change schools after Christmas.

It was lonely on the farm after living in Shagway, and Jimmie was glad when the Szep family had come to the tenant house in early spring. He and Laszlo had become instant friends.

Istvan[5] Szep and his wife Maria found English difficult.

Their oldest daughter, Margit, was shy. Jimmie wasn't sure he had ever heard her say much of anything. But she went to school—they all rode the same bus, even though she stayed on longer to reach the junior high school in Cherry Hill—so he knew she had to speak some English.

Laszlo said he had learned a lot of the language of Americans on the trains and the ship as they traveled from Europe to the United States, often translating words for his parents. Most of the time he sounded as if he'd always spoken English, except for the way he occasionally pronounced some of his vowels.

His younger sister Eniko wasn't old enough to go to school yet. She talked constantly, unlike Margit, and mixed Hungarian with English all the time in a crazy word puzzle that Jimmie could hardly figure out.

***

---

[5]Istvan. Steven, in Hungarian

The boys jumped from the truck and ran into the house. Maria Szep greeted them with a big smile. She was square and solid. Laszlo looked like her. "Come now, you have cookies and milk. Growing boys, yes? Wash. Sit." She pointed down the hallway.

Jimmie grinned at Laszlo, and they hurried to the bathroom to clean the dirt of the road from their hands. When they returned to the kitchen Mrs. Szep spun them around. "Faces too. *Siess, siess.*"[6]

At last they were seated at the kitchen table, and Margit pulled a sheet of hot sugar cookies from the oven. The sweet smell made Jimmie's stomach rumble and his mouth water. Mrs. Szep had already poured glasses of cold milk for the boys and her husband. Eniko was tied into a chair with a long towel so she wouldn't fall.

She was given a cookie first, and then a plateful was placed on the table. The males in the room all reached for the warm snack.

"Margit and I have treat later," she explained.

---

[6]say SHE-ahsh. Hurry up in Hungarian.

"When work is done. You men do good jobs today?"

"Boy and I deliver old hay bales to man for make better garden, across river." He winked at Laszlo. "New cutting is soon." He tilted his head toward Jimmie. "We pick up this one with broken bike on way home."

Jimmie stuffed his mouth with cookie to keep from laughing.

"Is good," Maria Szep said. "Jimmie, you come back ten June. Is Margit's Nameday. We have cake. Tell your mother."

Jimmie looked at Margit. She turned red and looked away.

"Like birthday, only is birthday of saint with same name," Mrs. Szep explained.

"Thank you. I'd like that very much," Jimmie said politely. Laszlo was already on his second cookie. Jimmie gulped down his milk and also grabbed a second golden circle.

"Out you go, now. Both you boys. Shoo, shoo. Go fix that bicycle."

4. HAZEL'S TEARS

Jimmie already knew the tire couldn't be fixed. He could see a jagged hole in it, and the tube was almost certainly ruined too. He'd be stuck near his house for days. At least until someone went into Cherry Hill to shop. And he wasn't sure he had enough money to buy the new parts.

With Laszlo's help he got the bicycle out of the truck and the boys walked it toward Jimmie's house. They dropped the bike in the yard and headed for the side door.

Mrs. Mosher wouldn't know they'd already had cookies, and maybe she'd offer them a treat too.

The kitchen door was propped open because of the warm weather, and the boys could see into the room through the screen door. It didn't look or smell as if there was any baking happening. Jimmie's mom, Hazel, was seated at the kitchen table with her head in her hands. Jed, her husband, stood on the other side of the table. He was talking.

The boys entered but more cautiously than they had originally planned. Adult conversations could be confusing. Sometimes they signaled trouble for everyone.

As they entered the room, Jimmie was shocked to discover that his mother was actually crying. Although she wasn't a bubbly person who laughed and made jokes all the time, Jimmie had rarely seen her cry.

She had cried when Dad had brought home a new electric washing machine. That was weird. But this didn't look like happy tears. She hadn't cried when they'd moved from her hometown of Shagway out to this farm. She'd only said quietly, "We'll do what we have to do, Jed. Your mother needs us there to take care of things." So what could make her more sad than moving away from her friends and family?

"Should I go home?" Laszlo whispered to Jimmie.

"No. Let's find out what's going on." Jimmie was glad to have a friend by his side.

Hazel, Jimmie's mom, raised her head and wiped her hands across her cheeks. She looked at

Jimmie and Laszlo and then up at Jimmie's dad. "We need to tell them," she said. "They all live here too."

"I agree." Jed nodded. "I'll go right over and tell Istvan and Maria so they hear the bad news from me personally, as soon as we explain things to the boys."

"What's wrong?" Jimmie asked. "Why is Mom crying?"

Jed Mosher said, "We've received a serious letter from the bank, son. They are saying the mortgage on this property was never fully paid and now we owe a huge sum of money because of interest. We may have to move."

"We moved before. Why would that be so bad?" Jimmie asked.

"We'd have nothing. The bank would take the house and all the land instead of the money. We couldn't buy another place. The Szeps would probably have to move, too."

Laszlo turned white. "We had no money left after my father paid for our passage to America. It's very hard when you don't know if you can get another meal. We had to eat weeds from the ditches and take dirty jobs no one else would do to get a few coins for milk. Sometimes a kind farmer would give us some eggs or wormy apples."

"Gosh, I didn't know," Jimmie said.

"I don't want to leave and live like that again. It would be awful if that happened to you," Laszlo said. He looked as if he might cry, too.

Mr. Mosher put an arm around Laszlo's shoulder. "Try not to worry. Let's go talk to your parents."

5. GRANNY MAY'S SONG

Things were no more cheerful the next day. There was supposed to be an official piece of paper that proved the house and land had been fully paid for, but Jed Mosher could not find it.

The paper wasn't in his father's file boxes where it belonged. It wasn't anywhere in the small room that had been used for an office for as long as anyone could remember.

Jed had asked his mother, Maybella, what might have happened to it. The problem with that plan was that Granny May could no longer remember things. She wasn't always in her right mind. She mostly sat in a rocking chair and muttered or sang to herself. During the colder months, her chair had been placed by a hot air register which brought heat from the furnace. Now that it was summer, she sat on the porch a lot.

She could help shuck peas or pick stems and bugs out of pails of berries Jimmie brought home.

But she wasn't good at answering questions.

Today, Granny May was in the living room, rocking and singing;

> Hey, hey, oh playmate,
> Come out and play with me
> And bring your dollies three.
> Climb up my apple tree.
> Jump in my rain barrel
> Slide down my cellar door,
> And we'll be jolly friends
> Forevermore, more, more.

When Jimmie had been small he thought this song was funny, but today it was just maddening. Why couldn't Granny remember where her husband, Jedediah, Senior, had kept such an important paper?

Jimmie was so annoyed he just wanted to get out of the house. No one had to remind him to do his chores. He angrily hoed the rows in the garden, taking out his frustration on the weeds that seemed to grow up overnight. He wondered how Laszlo's family had known which weeds were safe to eat. The baby vegetables were just starting to poke through the ground and he had to be careful not to cut those off by mistake. He knew what each of those plants looked like.

Next, he scattered cracked corn for the chickens in their pen. The birds came running to him, squawking and flapping their wings. Chickens were silly, but there were always eggs for breakfast and baking. He hunted through the nest boxes and found two white and four brown ones which he cradled in his shirt-tail and took to the kitchen.

There, he picked up a small bucket of food scraps and took it out back to the two pigs. They thought it was as good as sugar cookies. He scratched their backs as they snuffled through the trough of old cabbage leaves and potato peelings. He liked the pigs but knew better than to think of them as pets. In the fall they would go to be butchered and cut into pork chops and hams and bacon.

When Jimmie returned from the barnyard he found Cora Dubois and her mother in the kitchen, talking with his own mother. Small jars of bright red strawberry jam were lined up on the table.

"We picked the berries yesterday and made the jam last night," Cora said with pride.

"Thank you! We should have black raspberries to share in a week or so," said Hazel. "You kids can go play if your chores are done, Jimmie."

"They are, Mom." He turned to Cora, "Let's go."

Granny May could be heard from the living room, still singing in a high crackling voice, "Jump in my rain barrel, slide down my cellar door."

6. JIMMIE AND CORA

Jimmie liked Cora as a friend and was glad to see her. He could tell her about driving over the railroad bridge when they were alone.

Cora lived in the big white house just across the river. She was an only child, like Jimmie, and the same age. They rode the same school bus to the elementary school at Cherry Pit Junction. As soon as school had ended for the summer, the bridge—the cause of the adventure on Mr. Szep's "private" road—on East South River Road had been closed for repairs. When Jimmie saw Cora, he was reminded that her dad was the manager at the canning factory that was near the school. Having the bridge closed must make it really difficult for him to get to work.

"Come on," Jimmie urged Cora toward the kitchen door.

Cora held back. "Let's go see Granny May first."

"Aw, she's been singing that song all day."

"I want to hear it again," Cora insisted.

The friends went to the living room where Granny May was still rocking, smiling and singing.

"I know how to make this song more fun," Cora said.

"Really? How? We don't have a rain barrel, but we do have a cistern, a cellar door and apple trees. I'm fresh out of dolls, so if you want to act it out, you'll need to bring your own."

"I don't like dolls," Cora said, flipping her dark braids over her shoulders. "Hold up your hands, like this."

She extended her raised hands toward Jimmie, palms outward.

"Why am I doing this?" Jimmie askcd.

"You'll see."

Cora waited for Granny May to begin the song again and she sang along with her this time. The old lady smiled and nodded her head. She looked very happy.

Cora added motions to the words by clapping her own hands three times, then crossing hands and clapping each one, clapping her hands against Jimmie's, both fronts and backs.[7]

"Now you do it too," Cora instructed.

They clapped together until Jimmie got it right.

"Now faster," Cora said. "And I know a second verse too."

Jimmie and Cora clapped fast and Cora sang till they were both laughing. But when she got to the line in the second verse that went "My dolly's got the flu, Boo hoo hoo hoo hoo hoo," Jimmie dropped his hands and said, "That's just silly."

"So what? It's just for fun." Cora's dark eyes flashed.

Granny May apparently hadn't known the second verse because she had just been listening. Now she started in again, "Jump in my rain barrel, slide down my cellar door."

Cora looked at Granny and then at Jimmie. "Does she sing this song a lot?"

"Nope. I haven't heard it since I was a really little kid. Why?"

---

[7] see song and clapping instructions at the end of the book

"Because maybe your grandmother is remembering something but doesn't know how to tell us. Your mom told my mom and me about that missing paper."

The girl turned to Granny May. "Is that important? A rain barrel and a cellar door?"

The old lady continued to smile and nod but she didn't answer and she wasn't really looking at anyone. One of her teeth was missing, and it made her look a little frightening. Jimmie remembered her from before she'd been strange. Senile, his mother called it. He realized she wasn't actually scary, but he hardly knew who this person was.

"Jump in my rain barrel, slide down my cellar door," Granny May sang again, clapping her wrinkled hands together in time to the song.

7. BASEMENT OR CELLAR?

"Is a cellar the same thing as a basement?" Cora asked Jimmie.

"I guess so," he answered.

"Have your parents looked in the basement for that paper?"

"Probably not. It's small and dirty. I don't think anyone would put something important there."

"But it has a cellar door, right?"

"Sure, there's one inside and another outside with slanted doors that open to the hatchway steps. Hey! I'll bet there could have been a rain barrel by it a long time ago."

The friends ran outside and around the house to the back. Jimmie couldn't reach the handle on the big hatchway door and pull it open at the same time. He wasn't tall enough. But he slipped his hand under the bottom edge of the door and heaved it up and over on its hinges. The door settled with a thump on a padded post located in the right place to catch the door so the hinges wouldn't break.

Cora peered into the space where steps descended into gloom. "Are there lights down there?"

"There are a few bulbs with string pulls. I know where they are," Jimmie assured her.

Interesting odors arose as they went down the wide steps. Crates of potatoes had been placed at the edges of several steps for storage over the winter. Now it was almost the next summer and most of the ones that were left had white sprouts growing from them. Jimmie had helped cut some of these old potatoes into pieces and planted them in the garden just last week. They would turn into whole new plants.

There were large dark green squash that looked the same as they had the year before when they'd been placed in this cool storage area. A box of apples hadn't fared so well. The ones on top were all wrinkled, and Jimmie's nose twitched at the sharp aroma. He was pretty sure there must be some rotten ones at the bottom.

He'd ask his mom if that needed to be cleaned up. Maybe she would make applesauce with the ones that weren't rotting.

At the bottom was another door with a metal latch. Jimmie pressed a lever which lifted a bar and the door swung open with a creak. It was dark as night in the basement until Jimmie reached out and felt around. When his hand touched a string he pulled it, and a bare light bulb sparked to life.

Now he could see well enough to find the other strings. He went around and pulled them all.

Even with all the lights on there wasn't much to see. The main room was plain gray concrete with big stones showing at the top level. There were a few dingy windows right up next to where the ceiling should be, except there wasn't really a ceiling. You could see the edges of all the wooden joists that held up the floor of the house. What looked like a ceiling was really the underside of the floorboards of the kitchen.

"This is it?" Cora asked. She sounded disgusted.

8. CRAWLSPACE

"What did you expect? There's the furnace and the coal bin. It's pretty much empty this time of year. This space over here gets filled with split logs in fall because the furnace can burn wood, too. I used to help Grandpa stack it." He pointed straight ahead.

Tools and frying pans and baskets hung overhead. One whole corner of the basement looked as if it were walled off into another room with no door. Cora didn't need to ask what that was because her house had one too. It was a cistern that held water. When it rained, the water ran off the roof, through the eave troughs and downspouts, and collected in this concrete holding tank. It wasn't safe for drinking, but could be used for washing and cleaning. Just then the electric pump that carried the water up to the sinks and toilet kicked on. The noise was startling and Cora jumped.

Jimmie laughed. "Scaredy-cat!"

"I live by the river. Drop in," Cora replied with a saucy toss of her braids. She looked left and saw some shelves along the wall. They were partially filled with glass jars of green beans, corn, peaches, apples, tomatoes and pickles. "Hey, did your mom put these up?" she asked.

"Sure. Just because we only moved here this winter doesn't mean Mom doesn't know how to do things. We've always helped Granny May can things from garden. It's a lot of work."

"I know. My mother and I do it all summer long. Most things just got planted in the garden, but pretty soon the black raspberries will be ripe, and then the early peas we put in last month will be ready. After that, there are fruits and vegetables to take care of all summer and fall."

"But we sure eat good in the winter," Jimmie boasted.

"Well," Cora corrected him. "You eat well."

"If you say so. I guess we could look on the shelves, but there's not much space down here to hide anything."

Cora and Jimmie spent quite a while moving jars, feeling behind the shelves, and looking inside any boxes they found. Jimmie stacked up two potato crates to stand on so he could reach the baskets hanging from the rafters. There were no papers in any of them.

There was only one more place left to explore. The wall opposite the shelves didn't go all the way up to the beams. Above the wall was a dark narrow opening.

"That's the crawlspace under the living room," Jimmie explained. "There's no floor, just loose dirt. Grandpa only put a real basement under the kitchen. Probably because he had to dig the hole by hand."

"Let's get up there," Cora said. She was not the kind of girl that minded getting dirty. She always wore blue jeans or overalls except at school, where girls were required to wear skirts.

"We'll need flashlights," Jimmie said. "I have one in my bedroom. I'll see if I can find another. Do you think you can carry the ladder that's out by the corncrib? It's a short one."

"I'll get it," Cora promised.

9. A BURIED TREASURE?

A few minutes later, Cora and Jimmie returned to the basement and worked together to lean the ladder against the partial wall.

"I found a trowel too. With all that dirt, maybe we'll need it," Cora said.

She scrambled up and over the top of the concrete onto the dirt. There was very little space between it and the joists that supported the floor of the living room above it. Jimmie climbed the ladder and handed her one of the flashlights.

"This space is really tight; I can't even sit up," Cora said as she played the light around the crawlspace.

"Lots of cobwebs," Jimmie said. "You don't mind?"

"No. But I'll probably have to take a bath. Are you coming?"

"I'm right behind you," Jimmie assured her.

They inched forward on their bellies, pushing

the lights ahead of them. When Jimmie thought they were about halfway to the far wall, he said, "Stop here. Let's see if we need to go any farther. This is hard."

They played the beams of their flashlights into the far corners and around every edge of the area. All they saw was more dirt, cobwebs and wooden beams, nothing that could have held an important paper.

"This trowel hurts," complained Cora, wiggling and pulling the small shovel from the pocket of her overalls. "But I brought it up here; I'm going to try to find something. Maybe there's a buried treasure."

"Jeepers creepers! You think pirates lived here after my grandpa built it?" Jimmie scoffed.

Cora stuck the point of the trowel into the dry earth. She pulled it out and pushed it in again. The dirt was loose and the blade went deep, almost its full length. She pulled it out and tried a different place. After several tries, she rolled over.

"There's nothing here, Cora. Your mom will be wondering where you are."

But Cora didn't want to give up. She stabbed the trowel in again. There was a sound like metal hitting metal.

"Jimmie! Come around here and hold the light. I found something."

Cora tossed scoops of dirt away from her as quickly as she could in the tight quarters. Jimmie dug with his hands. Soon they uncovered a rusty round container.

"Aw, it's just an old tin can," Jimmie grumbled.

"There's more stuff here," Cora said. "Shine the light where I was digging."

As Jimmie did so, there was a flash of blue that dazzled their eyes.

"What was that?" he yelped.

Cora loosened some more dirt and brushed it away with her hand. Carefully, to keep from getting cut on its sharp edges, she tossed another can aside and then pulled a beautiful dark blue bottle from the hole. Something rattled inside it.

"Hey, I can feel ridges near the bottom. Hold the light still. It's words, I think. 'BRO-MO-CE-DIN,'" she sounded out. "'FOR

HEADACHES.' Some kind of medicine bottle."

"What's inside?" Jimmie asked.

Cora shook the bottle gently. "Hold out your hand." Two tarnished dimes fell into Jimmie's palm.

"Wow! Twenty cents. I only need a ninety-nine for a new bike tube."

"OK, you keep the money. Who cares about that? I want the blue bottle," Cora said. She smiled and rubbed it against her sleeve to remove the grime.

10. CORA'S DILEMMA

Without his bike, Jimmie stayed close to home, and Cora was grounded because she stained a good blouse and ripped her overalls digging with Jimmie.

They talked on the phone and decided the next basement they could look in was at Laszlo's house. "Your grandfather built that one too," Cora reminded Jimmie.

"Yes, and it's newer. I don't think there's any dirty crawlspace there. We can explore it after Margit's party."

***

Margit's party! Every child in the neighborhood had been invited. That meant Jimmie and Cora, and George and Ruby Harris who lived halfway up Mulberry Hill, beyond Cora's house. Of course Margit's siblings, Laszlo and Eniko, would be there. No one Margit's age lived nearby.

The daisies were in full bloom and Cora picked

a handful. They looked lovely in her new-to-her but old blue bottle. It would make a nice present for Margit. Mrs. Szep had said that flowers were a good gift for girls.

But Cora had given up a lot to get that bottle. The twenty cents she claimed she didn't care about was almost as much as the quarter she received each week for doing household chores, and she'd had to spend days at home because of the damaged clothes. She didn't want to give the blue glass away.

In her mind, Cora handed the bottle full of flowers to Margit a hundred times and took it back again just as many. Could she really give up her treasure? She didn't want to be selfish, but hadn't she found it? Maybe Margit would think it was nothing special and throw the bottle away after the flowers wilted. Then no one would have it.

***

The days dragged by, but June tenth finally came. Mr. Dubois agreed to drive the three children who lived east of the river to the party even though it was a long way around on other roads because the bridge was closed. Cora's father, Philippe Dubois, was a sensible man who did not use a railroad bridge as a road.

Mr. Dubois pulled up in front of the unpainted tenant house. He said he'd return for them in three hours, and the friends burst from the car. Cora ran to knock on the door, but George and Ruby hung back. Although they knew Laszlo from school and they saw Margit on the bus, they had never visited the Szep's home. Maybe they had been included only because it was polite to invite neighbors.

11. GEORGE AND RUBY

Laszlo opened the door. "Come in! We decorated."

The living room was criss-crossed overhead with twisted streamers of crepe paper. Kitchen chairs were arranged in a circle with balloons tied to their backs. The children placed their wrapped gift packages on a small table. Jimmie stood behind Laszlo, and he batted a loose balloon at George. "Don't let it touch the floor!"

George tipped it to Cora, who managed to bump it upwards, but an air current caught the balloon and pushed it down.

"You lose," Laszlo teased.

Just then, Margit and Eniko entered the room. Eniko ran to Ruby. Ruby was seven and petite, the closest in age and size to Laszlo's little sister.

Eniko put her hand on Ruby's arm. "Dark. Why dark?" she asked.

"Hush, it's not nice to say things like that," said Margit, turning red and picking up the toddler.

"It's OK," said George.

"She's never seen a Negro," Margit explained.

Ruby took a step toward the sisters and touched Eniko's leg where it dangled below Margit's arm. "Just because. That's how we were born. My skin feels the same as yours, only it's browner."

"Down," Eniko commanded.

Margit put the little girl on the floor.

"Play with me," Eniko said to Ruby, grabbing her hand and pulling her toward the door.

All the children ran outside where Margit took a stick and scratched a hopscotch board in the dirt of the driveway. George added the numbers, drawing them carefully. He liked math, and although he thought of this as a girl's game, the geometric pattern of the squares appealed to him.

Cora took the first turn and threw a stone onto square one. She successfully hopped through the course, but when she picked up the stone on the way back Margit said, "You have to put it on your head."

"Why?" Cora asked. This was a rule she'd never

heard.

"That's the way we played in Hungary, and it's my party," Margit said.

Cora tried to hop and keep the stone on her head, but her hair was straight and smooth. The stone slid off.

Jimmie and Laszlo took turns. Laszlo's stiff short hair helped hold the rock in place. Ruby won, though, because the stone nestled into her dark curls and didn't budge. George had the same black curly hair, but his was buzzed close to his head for summer.

"Let's play hide-and-seek. That tree is home base," Laszlo said, pointing. He touched Jimmie. "You're it. You have to count to fifty."

Everyone scattered while Jimmie leaned against the tree and covered his eyes. "One, two, three..."

If someone was spotted they tried to run to the home base tree before being tagged by the person who was "it." They played this game the longest.

George yelled "safe" for the third time as he touched the tree. No one else managed to avoid being tagged so many times.

Just then, Mrs. Szep called from the door. "Come in, *gyermekek*,[8] we have cake and presents now."

---

[8]say GYER-ma-kek, children in Hungarian

12. MARGIT'S PRESENTS

After they were all settled in the living room, Mrs. Szep served squares of a rich cake layered with chocolate and caramel, giving Margit a piece first in honor of her celebration.

Jimmie had never tasted anything quite like this special treat.

"Mama made it three days ago," Margit explained. "It's better that way because the flavors blend."

At last it was time for the presents. Eniko was too young to understand that the gifts weren't for her, so Mrs. Szep coaxed her into the kitchen with a promise of an extra glass of grape Koolaid.

Laszlo handed a small box wrapped in newspaper comics to his sister. She tore the paper off and found two packages of seeds. One was for snapdragon flowers and the other for carrots.

"Something pretty to look at, and something good to eat," Margit said. "Thank you, Laszlo."

Ruby had found a smooth rock to give Margit,

reddish in color with a gray stripe. "It's really pretty when it's wet," she explained.

Jimmie had felt a responsibility to bring something nice even though the children had been told the gifts should be small tokens. After all, his dad owned all the land and both houses. Except for Margit, he was also the oldest. But he hadn't been able to get to town to buy anything in a store. Instead he had washed dishes for his mother every night for the past week to earn this gift. As he handed a package wrapped in red tissue paper to Margit, he said, "Be careful and don't break it."

"It's heavy!" Margit said. She carefully peeled away the paper and found a pint canning jar filled with Mrs. Mosher's famous pickled peaches. "Oh Jimmie; thank you. They're so golden, and I've heard how wonderful they taste. We'll save them for Sunday dinner."

Jimmie smiled, satisfied that he'd brought something worthy.

Only George and Cora were left. "You go first," Cora said.

"OK. I made this myself, Margit. I hope you

won't think it's just for little kids," George said.

His present was also small. When Margit opened it, she wasn't sure what she was looking at. There was a piece of a branch about six inches long in the box and that was all. It had a notch in the top. She picked it up. "What is it?"

"Blow in that slanted end," George said.

Margit did, and a shrill whistle came from the hole. Eniko ran in from the kitchen, shrieking and clapping.

"Now I can call you little kids in for supper," Margit said, giving Laszlo a playful push.

"Hey!" Laszlo yelled. But he said to George, "That's really cool. Will you show me how to make one?"

"Sure, if you have a knife. It's just a willow stem."[9]

Finally it was Cora's turn. There was one box left on the table, and it was round and about a foot tall—bright pink and green. Cora had found a piece of wrapping paper that said "Happy

---

[9]see instructions to make a willow whistle at the end of the book

Birthday" on it in the back closet at her house. It was supposedly Saint Margit's birthday, not her neighbor's, but this was the best she could do.

Laszlo laughed. "It's an oatmeal box. She's brought you breakfast, Margit."

Margit reached for the gift.

"Don't tip it!" Cora sounded alarmed.

The beautiful blue bottle filled with fresh daisies was inside, surrounded by a twist of newspaper at the bottom to keep the glass from shifting.

"I love it," Margit exclaimed when she had carefully removed the bouquet from the box, and she gave Cora a little hug. The girls smiled at each other.

"The water was fresh this morning, but you can always pick more daisies when these wilt." Cora said.

"Let's go back outside," Jimmie said, looking at the clock on the mantle. "We've got a whole hour before Cora's dad comes."

"You children go play." Margit dismissed them in her most superior voice. "Thank you for coming, and for my gifts."

"You're welcome," everyone chorused. But Laszlo stuck his tongue out at Margit as soon as her back was turned.

13. KING OF THE HILL

"Race you to that hump on the edge of my lawn," Jimmie yelled.

"You're on," George agreed.

But Ruby grabbed her brother's shirt and complained. "That's not fair. I'm too little to ever beat you in a race."

"Aw, come on, Ruby. You won the hopscotch. I need to get the kinks out."

George pulled away and took off running, in a hopeless effort to catch Jimmie and Laszlo, who now had a significant head start.

Ruby looked at Cora, who shrugged her shoulders, but didn't run away.

Laughing, the girls held hands and skipped in the direction of Jimmie's house. They reached the small hill only a minute behind the boys who were already lying in the fresh June grass, panting hard from their sprint.

Ruby walked to the top of the green mound that rose oddly from the edge of the trimmed lawn. Just past the hump, the ground angled gently downwards ending at a weedy strip that separated the mowed area from a tiny creek. "I'm king of the hill-ill," she suddenly sang out and threw herself flat on her stomach.

"That's cheating," Laszlo said. "You have to stand up."

"Says who?" Ruby taunted. "I need an advantage since I'm the youngest."

Jimmie and George picked Ruby up by her arms and legs and carried her off the hill, but Cora saw an opportunity, and raced to the top.

"Now I'm king," she announced.

Laszlo gave her a firm push. "Not for long."

Just in time, Cora remembered that she was wearing party clothes. She'd get in trouble again for sure if she ended up with grass stains on her skirt. "Darn dresses," she said, side-stepping so she wouldn't fall. "I can't play this game."

"Well, what can you do?" Jimmie asked.

"I thought we were going to explore Laszlo's basement," she answered.

"Why?" Laszlo said. "It's just full of empty canning jars and junk. We haven't lived here long enough yet to even clean it out."

Cora perked up. "That's perfect. We need to find something really old, where nobody's looked for a long time."

Laszlo and Cora explained to George and Ruby the problem the Mosher family was facing and the need to find the paper that proved they'd finished paying for the house.

George said it wasn't very sensible to think that a song Granny May liked on one day weeks ago was a clue.

Cora's face got red. "I suppose you've got a better idea, then? We can't just let the bank take Jimmie's house away. Laszlo's too."

George shook his head and held his tongue.

Jimmie defended Cora. "Granny can't get her thoughts together, but she sings things she wants to say. Sometimes she pats me on the head as if I were still a little boy and sings 'Tell me why the sky's so blue, and I will tell you just why I love you.'"

Everyone nodded sympathetically. Old people could be hard to understand.

"Maybe I can borrow an apron from Margit,"

Cora said. "I can't ruin this dress or my mom will be really mad."

"My dad's got old work shirts hanging in the back porch we can borrow. They'll cover you and Ruby up better than anything," Laszlo said. "It's too bad girls are stuck wearing dresses."

"Not when I have a choice," Cora said firmly.

With a chorus of "Let's go," and "Hooray," they all ran in the direction of the tenant house.

14. THE SECOND CELLAR

Similar to the Mosher's place, the tenant house had an outside entrance to the basement with a slanting wood hatchway door. Jimmie and George opened this while Laszlo found two large shirts for the girls to wear.

The one Ruby put on fell almost to her ankles and even the short sleeves covered most of her arms.

"You'll stay clean!" Cora said. She wasn't swallowed quite so completely in Mr. Szep's shirt, but her dress was protected and that was all that mattered.

"What about light?" George asked.

The friends entered the cellar and glanced at the dusty, cobweb filled space. There were more windows than they expected, all high and small, above ground level, and the late afternoon sun shot yellow rays through the gloom and drew hot rectangles on the floor. They saw the furnace, coal bin, cistern, and steps leading up to the interior of the house; these were ordinary. But it didn't look as if there were extra closets or secondary rooms.

Jimmie grabbed a broom that was propped near the door and swung it from side to side, clearing a path through the webs.

Laszlo found the string for the light and pulled it on. The bare bulb glowed but didn't help much. "Cora, you and Ruby go check out those canning jars and stuff." He flexed a muscle. "We men will move the boxes and wood."

After a few minutes of noisy swiping, shoving, carrying and poking, the door from the upstairs opened and Mrs. Szep's anxious voice floated down, "Who is there, please? What you do?"

"It's just us, Mom. We're, uh, cleaning for you," Laszlo yelled.

"Such nice children! I give you more Koolaid when you get tired." The door closed.

"That was close," George said.

Cora made an impatient sound, "She wouldn't have any idea what we're really doing, even if she came down here."

"What are we doing?" Ruby asked. "I don't really know what to look for."

"An old paper. Something that looks important," Jimmie said. "It might have been put somewhere that seemed safe."

"OK," Ruby said, but she didn't sound as if she understood.

George pulled something from a box and said, "Aha!"

Everyone rushed over to him. "What?"

He held a metal tape measure. "I'm going to check the size of the inside and compare it to the outside of the house. Maybe there's a secret room. That would be a good place to put important papers. Ruby, come help me hold the other end."

Jimmie and Laszlo kept searching through boxes and crates and restacking firewood. Cora found some rags and wiped the canning jars clean, arranging them neatly on the wooden shelves with the raised words to the front. Some were marked "Kerr," or "Presto," but most of them had the word "Ball." She put all the smaller ones together, then the medium ones and the large ones, becoming so focused on her task she almost forgot to check for a piece of paper that might have been sealed inside. Almost, but not quite.

She really wanted to help save Jimmie's house.

In a few minutes George and Ruby appeared. "It's the same outside and inside," George said, shaking his head. "I don't think there's any secret room."

"Makes sense," Laszlo added. "You can see windows all around the outside walls."

"Let's go wash up and have that drink your mom promised before Cora's dad comes," Jimmie said.

15. DISCOURAGED AND PURPLE

A few mornings later, Cora rode her bicycle to Jimmie's house, and they followed the tiny creek south and upstream through the woods. Jimmie had tied two empty tin pails to his belt, and Cora carried last-year's school lunchbox containing two sandwiches, cookies, and a thermos bottle full of lemonade.

When they reached the railroad tracks, where the trees had been cut back and there was more sunlight, berry bushes grew tall.

"The blackcaps should be ripe," Jimmie said. "I checked a few days ago, and they were already red."

Cora arrived at the line of thorny black raspberry plants and set the lunchbox on the ground. "Perfect. And more than just the top one in each cluster is ready. We should be able to get lots to take home."

"Pie!" Jimmie said, his mouth watering.

"Too many seeds. I'd rather have jelly," Cora

answered.

"Plain, with cold milk."

"Fresh. Right now." Cora pulled dark purple berries off a bush and filled her mouth. She wore patched blue jeans and an old blouse. There would be no worries about keeping her clothes clean today, which was good because berry juice made stains that never came out.

Jimmie wore jeans and a striped t-shirt as he did almost every day in the summer.

They picked berries and tried to fill their pails although quite a few of the delicious fruits ended up in their stomachs.

"Ouch!" Cora said when she got snagged again on a thorn and the scratch bled. "I should have worn long sleeves."

"And I'm hot. Let's have some lemonade," Jimmie suggested.

They sat on a fallen log and Cora filled the thermos cup. "We'll have to share," she said.

"That's OK. You don't have cooties."

"Thanks."

"You're better than most girls. They're always fussing about their hair and stuff."

Cora took in this information without answering. She didn't understand other girls very well either. She unwrapped a sandwich and handed half to Jimmie. "It's peanut butter."

"Yum."

"I've been thinking," Cora said. "George is probably right that it's silly to think we can find that mortgage paper."

Jimmie nodded. "Yeah, I don't know any other basements to look in."

"Where did Granny May come from, before she married your grandfather?"

"Her family's house is in Cherry Hill. My great-uncle owns it now."

"So, could we get in the basement?"

"I guess so, but we'd have to get to town. My bike is still out of commission and it's a long ride anyway. Even longer for you. Give me another half-sandwich. Please," he added.

Cora peeled the wax paper away from the other square of bread and peanut butter. There was a red layer beside the brown. "This one has jelly! Maybe on shopping day you could go to your uncle's."

"Maybe. I'd have to tell my nosy cousins what I was doing. They'd probably spill the beans and we'd get told to butt out. Besides, why would Grandpa and Granny take important papers to that house?"

"I don't know. Grown-ups do weird things."

With that settled, Jimmie and Cora finished the sandwiches and the lemonade. Instead of the cookies, they ate more berries for dessert.

After that, they worked hard to fill their buckets and didn't talk much. Cora topped hers off first, and then she helped Jimmie. By mid-afternoon they were hot and sweaty but had two full pails. They followed the creek back toward Jimmie's house, walking slowly. It would be a disaster to trip and spill the fruit they'd worked so hard to pick.

Jimmie's mother welcomed and praised them for the full berry buckets, and she filled tall glasses with refreshing ice water. She chuckled at their purple faces and hands, suggesting they wash while she packed half the berries in a container with a lid. Cora placed this in her bicycle basket.

"See you later, alligator." Cora grinned as she mounted her bike.

"After a while, crocodile," Jimmie answered. He waved as she rode away.

16. FORTY-THREE CENTS

The next day was Friday. Shopping day in Cherry Hill would be Saturday. Jimmie knew he could go to town with his parents if he asked. He could also stay home if he preferred. The Szeps were nearby if anything happened that required an adult.

But he couldn't decide if he wanted to ride along. He sat on top of that funny hump at the edge of the lawn, put his back to the road, and thought about the problem.

If he didn't go, there would be no chance at all to look in Uncle Marvin's basement. But he wasn't sure they'd visit the relatives, and he couldn't think of a good reason to ask his parents to stop there.

If he went, it would be really hard not to spend some of the money he did have on candy and a comic book. He had the twenty cents Cora found and gave him, and another thirty-six cents he'd saved. This still wasn't enough for the bike tube he needed. That cost a penny less than a dollar. It would take weeks to save that much unless he could do extra chores for money. He received twenty cents a week for feeding the chickens and pigs, hoeing, and carrying drinking water from the barn pump.

He tried to add the numbers in his head. Thirty-six plus twenty were fifty-six. That was easy. Subtracting that from ninety-nine cents was harder. But he thought he still needed forty-three cents. More than two weeks yet! If he got lucky he might find the three pennies somewhere. That was another good reason to go to town. People sometimes dropped money on the sidewalk by accident.

And that would cover only the tube. Maybe he could cut a piece of old rubber and make a boot to slip behind the big hole in the tire, although that would bump every time the wheel went around and probably wouldn't stay in place.

He was so lost in thought he didn't hear the person sneaking up behind him. Laszlo poked him in the ribs. "Gotcha!"

"Hey!" Jimmie yelled and jumped. Not only

was he startled but he was ticklish, and this prank really annoyed him. He spun around, ready to punch the person behind him. Just in time, he saw it was Laszlo, who was now doubled over with laughter.

Jimmie tackled his friend and they rolled over and over, wrestling. Before long, they landed at the bottom of the hill and barely avoided falling into the creek.

"What's up?" Laszlo asked. "You sure were thinking hard."

Jimmie explained about needing money so he could leave his yard without walking. He also told Laszlo about his great-uncle Marvin's basement being a possible place to search for the mortgage paper.

"I don't know. Would your grandfather think that a basement in town was safer than out here? Hey, maybe the basement here was really wet that year. Does this creek or the river flood? Maybe the paper isn't in any cellar." Laszlo was full of ideas.

"I've never seen the river get that high. This creek is nothing. It dries up in August. But I'll ask my dad if the basement ever flooded. That's a good idea," Jimmie said.

Laszlo pointed up the little hill. "We should build a fort on top of that."

17. THE ACCIDENT

Jimmie decided to stay home. He and Laszlo agreed that a fort was a great idea. There was lots of old lumber around the barn and outbuildings.

After asking Jimmie's mother, they phoned Cora, and George and Ruby to ask if they could come over after their chores were done.

George was the only one who had trouble getting permission. His father ran a bait shop on weekends at the edge of Thousand Lakes State Forest, and he was expected to help. In exchange for a promise to dig lots of nightcrawlers instead, Mr. Harris agreed to let the boy play with his friends on Saturday.

Jimmie's parents left for town before lunch. Early in the afternoon, the girls and George dropped their bikes in the Mosher's yard.

The boys pulled boards and two-by-fours to the small hill while Cora and Ruby brought hammers, saws, a level, and a can of rusty nails from one of the sheds.

"I got the post-hole digger," George said. He was carrying a heavy tool that looked like two skinny shovels hinged together. "We can put in good solid corner posts, and then fasten a sill to them to hold the floor. That way we can get off the ground. 'Cause it's not very flat."

"Good idea," Laszlo said.

"But the buried wood will rot in the dirt," Cora pointed out.

"Oh, phooey," Jimmie said. "Not this year. Maybe not even next year. That's good enough."

"Is this going to be our clubhouse?" Ruby asked.

"It sure is. We can find some old chairs and stuff to furnish it," Laszlo said.

Cora clapped her hands. "Let's make it two stories high so we have a lookout tower."

Farm life guaranteed that even at their ages the children had a general idea of how to build a structure. They laid out the heaviest boards, the ones that would hold up the floor, in a rectangle so they could see how large the clubhouse could be. It was smaller than they had hoped, but still big enough they all fit inside the borders with room to sit in a circle.

To make square corner posts they had to nail two-by-fours together.

Jimmie was allowed to have all the nails he wanted as long as they had been previously used. This meant it took time to straighten each bent nail enough that it could be pounded in again. There were two hammers, so Cora took one and carefully rolled the nails on a concrete block and tapped the shafts to take out the bends. She put the straight ones in another can, ready for use. Ruby held the boards tight and Jimmie hammered them together.

George marked the sill boards and cut them to the correct lengths. Meanwhile, Laszlo began digging one of the corner holes. He was a barrel-chested boy and very strong for his size.

He would thrust the post-hole digger into the ground, then pull the two handles apart. This made the shovel ends pinch together. He had to lift the tool out of the hole while holding the handles tight, or the dirt would drop out.

"How deep do we have to go?" he asked. "I'm

down about eighteen inches. The deeper I go the harder it gets."

"I'm not sure," Jimmie said. He paused and turned his attention back to the nail he was pounding. "Maybe two feet if we want a tower."

Just then Lazslo yelled.

Jimmie looked up, but his friend was gone.

18. THE SECRET CELLAR

They all dropped their tools or boards and ran to the spot where Laszlo had been digging. Jimmie reached out an arm and stopped Ruby just in time to prevent her from falling into the same hole that had swallowed Laszlo. The edges had collapsed beyond the shovel marks.

Jimmie lay down at the edge of the opening, stuck his head in and called, "Are you all right?"

The sun was beginning to angle from the west, and it illuminated a small spot about eight feet below the ground. They could see Laszlo's legs. He rolled over, so they knew he was alive, but he didn't make a sound.

"Come on," Cora said, grabbing Ruby's hand. "I know where the flashlights are." They ran toward the house.

Laszlo groaned and tried to sit up.

"He's hurt bad," George said.

"No, no I'm not." Laszlo's voice floated up to them, but it sounded faint. "I had... the wind...

knocked out of me. Wow." He panted hard. "I thought that was just an expression, but it's real. I think I'm OK, other than that."

"What's down there?" Jimmie asked.

Just then, the girls returned with two flashlights and a ball of string. "I'll send one down to him," Cora said.

She lowered a light through the hole until Laszlo grabbed hold of it. Jimmie took the other one and began shining it around the space, but he couldn't see anything from above except a dirt floor.

Laszlo, however, was exploring. "Hey, this is sort of like a cellar with no building over it. There are all kinds of jars with zinc lids, and little barrels. It looks really old."

"But how did people get in?" George asked.

"There's a door," Laszlo said. He started banging on something that sounded like wood. "Over here."

The children followed the sound, and scurried down the bank into the weeds. The hill did seem to be a little flatter on that side, although they hadn't noticed it before.

Jimmie ran to get a shovel, and everyone else started pulling weeds out of the side of the mound with their hands.

"Stand back," Jimmie said. He raised the shovel and thrust it into the hill. The blade went in about three inches and hit wood. Jimmie's teeth rattled with the impact.

"That's the door," Laszlo yelled. "Wait a minute. Let me try to pull on it. It opens in."

"We'll push," Cora called back.

Jimmie took charge, and first used the shovel to skim the dirt and remaining weeds away from the outside of the door.

They could hear Laszlo banging and rattling things on the other side. "The latch is rusted shut," he said. "Throw down a hammer."

"I can do that," Ruby said. She hurried away to find the tool.

A few minutes later, much of the outer surface of the door was revealed. Laszlo was now pounding on the metal catch more effectively.

The latch broke free with a loud clank.

"Now push," Jimmie said.

It was jammed, but in less than a minute, the

old door creaked inward as they pushed, and Laszlo pulled, with all their strength. Suddenly, whatever was stuck gave way, and the door opened all at once. Laszlo was thrown backwards from the force. Three steps led down into the dark space where Laszlo had fallen again. He looked surprised.

Laszlo scrambled out into the sunshine and joined his friends. They stared into the old cellar and played their flashlights across the shelves filled with boxes, bottles, jugs and crocks.

19. THE HIDEOUT

"What's going on here?" Jed Mosher called. Jimmie's parents had returned from shopping, but no one heard them arrive. The children had been completely focused on exploring the cave-like cellar.

"Uh, oh. Are we going to be in trouble?" George asked.

Jimmie shrugged. He wasn't sure.

"Well, well. I see you kids found the old root cellar." Mr. Mosher stuck his head in through the door.

"We, uh, Laszlo..."

Laszlo elbowed Jimmie in the ribs.

"Were you trying to build a fort? Seems to me like this would make a better clubhouse," Mr. Mosher said.

"Hot dog, Dad! Could we really do that?"

Ruby and Cora hugged each other. George grinned.

"Sure. As you can tell, no one uses it any more.

Your mother might want the jars and kitchen stuff. But you'll have to clean it out. Oh, and patch the roof." Jed Mosher laughed and pointed upwards; he didn't sound upset.

"What about the little barrels? They'd be good to sit on," Laszlo said.

"Those are called kegs. I don't see any problem with that. Hardly anyone stores things in barrels nowadays. I'll leave you to it. Mind, you put those tools and the wood away before you start working in here."

"We will," everyone said together.

"It's almost suppertime. When are your friends supposed to be home?" Mr. Mosher added, looking in the direction of Cora and George who were standing side by side.

"Leaping lizards!" George said. "Can we... may I use the phone?"

"Me, too," Cora echoed.

Ruby added, "No wonder my tummy is growling."

Mr. Mosher chuckled. "Come on in the house. Maybe I have a better idea."

The children followed Jimmie's dad around to

the kitchen side of the house. He pulled open the screen door.

"Hazel! Do you think you could rustle up enough food for all these young'ns if I get permission from their parents for them to stick around a little longer? They've got a job to finish up."

Jimmie's mother put her hands on her hips. "What kind of mischief have they gotten into? I knew we shouldn't have left Jimmie here alone."

"Nothing bad now, Mother. Just simmer down," Jed said. "They started a project that might have been a tad bit too big for them, but they found the old root cellar. There's a mess they need to clean up before nightfall, but a good meal would make that go a lot easier."

"I suppose I might be able to find enough tomato soup, and I can make grilled cheese sandwiches," she said, gently pulling Jimmie's ear.

Mr. Mosher said, "Come with me, Ruby. The phone's in my office. Let's call your parents." He nodded at Cora. "You'll be next. And Laszlo, you run home and tell your mother you'll be eating supper here."

"This is turning out really well," George whispered to Cora.

"Not unless the mortgage paper is in that cellar," Cora retorted quietly but fiercely. "What good is a clubhouse if the Moshers lose the whole farm?"

20. LIGHT AND SHADOW

The kitchen table wasn't large enough for everyone to sit down at once, so the children ate first. Jed Mosher wanted them to have plenty of daylight to clean up the lumber and tools that were now scattered all over the yard.

"Hurry, so we have time to explore our new hideout," Jimmie urged.

George and Laszlo wrestled all the large pieces of wood to the piles beside the barn, while Cora and Ruby picked up tools. Jimmie knew best where they belonged so he put them away in the shed that served as a workshop as the girls brought them to him. It wasn't nearly as much fun as getting everything out had been.

When they finished, Jimmie's dad inspected their work. Cora was holding her breath, afraid they might have to fix the hole in the lawn that same evening, and they wouldn't have time to look for the mortgage paper. But Jed said he was proud of them for doing such a good job. Cora let out a huge woosh of relief.

"Let's go!" she yelled.

Everyone raced for the door in the hillside. But it was already quite dark in the root cellar.

"May we use the kerosene lantern, if we're careful?" Jimmie yelled.

"Yes, just don't be showing off and knock it over," said his dad.

Jimmie ran to the workshop and came back a minute later with the lantern and a box of matches. "It's full," he said, shaking it gently and listening to the sound of the fuel in the tank.

Cora squinted at the glass. "The globe is clean."

"I know about lanterns, too," said George. "The wick looks trimmed, so that's good."

Jimmie carefully struck a match while George pressed the lever that lifted the globe so the wick could be lit. He set the lantern on a sturdy keg so it couldn't easily tip over and start a fire.

The air was cool and slightly moist in the old root cellar. There wasn't much dust, and only a few cobwebs hung in the highest recesses of the ceiling. The lantern light threw huge shadows of the children curving and bending around the

crockery and kegs. A reflection of the flame danced in every glass jar.

Ruby shivered. "I don't want to stay here very long. It's sort of spooky."

"We don't have much time anyway." George said. "We'll have to start riding home before eight."

While they had been putting the tools away they agreed the first thing to do was to search the cellar thoroughly. Cora still had hopes of finding the paperwork to prove the mortgage had been paid off. The others weren't as confident, but it couldn't hurt to look.

George said, "Let's clear one side of the room. Then as we check each box or whatever, we'll move it to that side so we know it's empty."

"Good idea, Cora said."

The older children didn't quite want to admit their feelings, but it was unnerving to have their shadows jumping wildly around them as they worked.

21. SOMETIMES SMALLER IS BETTER

All the food had been removed when the room had been last closed, so there were no rotten messes. A root cellar could keep potatoes, apples, squash and other vegetables like carrots and parsnips safe to eat for months, but not decades.

At dinner, Jimmie's dad had explained that no one had used it since he was a boy, when an icebox had been purchased for the kitchen in the house. And the icebox had eventually been replaced with an electric refrigerator. No one needed the root cellar at all, after that.

Almost every container was empty, but there was one box Jimmie opened that was full. After he lifted the lid, he called, "Cora, come here—you'll like this."

The box contained twelve of the beautiful blue bottles, duplicates of the one she had decided to give to Margit.

Cora gasped. "Do you think I could have one to

keep?" she said.

"I don't know why not. We'll ask," Jimmie said.

They continued to look inside every crock, keg, and box. They could see through the glass jars without moving them. There really wasn't much to find: a few clay flowerpots, a pair of worn-out shoes, two rusty rat traps, and the blue bottles.

"I quit," Ruby said, sitting down beside the shelves farthest from the door. "There's nothing else here, I'm getting cold, and we have to bicycle home yet. You big kids are too serious. This isn't fun any more."

"Aw, grow up, Ruby, if you want to play with us," George said. He sounded more annoyed than he was.

"Don't pick on her." Laszlo came to Ruby's defense. "She is the smallest, and she never complained once until now. I'm tired too."

All the children were tired and getting grumpy.

Ruby sighed and leaned against the wall. She just barely fit into the space between the shelving sections and was hidden in the shadows except for her bare legs sticking out straight in front of her. "Ouch," she yelled, and jumped up. "Something poked me in the back."

George's response showed how much he really cared for his little sister. He ran to her side and lifted her blouse to look. "Did something bite you? Are you OK? Well, there's no blood, anyway."

"What was it?" Cora asked. She knelt down and looked at the wall where Ruby had been sitting.

"Let me! I'm the one that got poked," Ruby said, wiggling in front of Cora. "Wow, there's something here, and it's got a knob. It sticks out just enough that I felt it." She tugged, and a long, narrow metal drawer pulled out of the wall.

22. SAVING THE FARM

"There's a skinny cardboard folder tied with string!" Ruby said in surprise.

"My dad uses those for important papers. It's called a document file," Cora corrected. She started to reach for it, and then changed her mind. "Jimmie you should open it. This is your farm."

Jimmie carried the file closer to the lantern. They all crowded around him as he untied the cord that turned out to be fastened to the cardboard so it couldn't get lost.

"There's a bunch of stuff in here," he said. He pulled out the papers and handed the empty folder to Laszlo. The first thing he unfolded was a paper with a fancy design around the edges. "This is really old. Oh, wow. It says Maybella Irene Morton was... something... baptized, I think... on May 22, 1872."

Cora was twitching. In fact she was practically jumping up and down. "It's the family's secret place to keep important stuff. I knew it! I knew we'd find it!"

"What else is there?" George asked.

Jimmie unfolded another paper. He began to leap around and pump his fist in the air. In fact, George was so alarmed at Jimmie's behavior he grabbed the lantern to steady it.

"She was right. Granny May was trying to tell us something. We've got to go show my mom." He ran out the door and everyone followed. But George lagged behind. He carefully blew out the lantern before leaving.

"Dad, Mom, come quick" Jimmie yelled as he ran.

The front door of the house opened. It was closest to the root cellar. "What's wrong, son?" Jed stuck his head out.

Everyone barreled onto the porch. George caught up just in time to hear Cora say, "We found it, Mr. Mosher. We found it!"

Jimmie handed the paper to his father and stood quietly while the man read it.

"Hazel. Hazel! Come see what these children have done." Jimmie's dad removed his glasses and wiped a hand across his eyes.

Mrs. Mosher came running from the kitchen. "Who's hurt? What's the matter?" she demanded.

With shaking hands Jed showed the yellowing document to his wife. Her eyes got wide. "You did this? All of you?"

"It was Ruby," Cora said. "She found the secret drawer."

"It was Cora," George said. "She wouldn't let us give up."

"It was Laszlo," Ruby said. "He fell in the cellar."

"Don't tell them that part," everyone said at once. But the grownups were too excited to be angry.

"It was Jimmie and George," Laszlo said. "They did the hard work moving things."

"It was really Granny May," Jimmie said. "She remembered the drawer in the old cellar, but she couldn't remember how to tell us."

Cora burst out singing, "Jump in my rain barrel, slide down my cellar door, and we'll be jolly friends forevermore."

***

And just in case you're wondering, Mr. Mosher gave Cora and the Harrises rides home in his car since it was well past eight o'clock.

On Monday morning, the Moshers took all the children to Cherry Hill. They marched into the bank as a group and presented the proof that the mortgage had been paid in full many years before. Nobody was going to have to move away.

Their next stop was the hardware store where a new tube and tire were purchased for Jimmie's bicycle. Mr. Mosher also bought each child a gift. Laszlo picked out a new pocket knife, and George selected a compass. Ruby found a small doll bed in the toy section that she liked.

But Cora chose a new notebook and pencil. "I'm going to make a list of all the interesting things we found. The blue bottle will be item number one." she said.

Then they went to the soda fountain at the drugstore and had ice cream. Two scoops each.

Hey, Hey, Oh Playmate

1. Hey, Hey, Oh Playmate   Come out and play with me,
2. Hey, Hey, Oh Playmate   I cannot play with you,

and bring your dollies three, climb up my apple tree.
my dolly's   got the flu,   boo hoo hoo hoo hoo hoo

Jump in my rain barrel,   slide down my cellar door,
Ain't got no rain barrel,   ain't got no cellar door,

and we'll be jolly friends   for   ever   more, more, more.
but we'll be jolly friends   for   ever   more, more, more.

key to
symbols

There are dozens of versions of this old folk song. They
are all correct, because folk songs are changed by people to
fit the occasion.

WILLOW WHISTLE

KNOW HOW TO USE A KNIFE SAFELY, AND GET PERMISSION!

FIND WILLOW GROWING NEAR WATER. IT HAS NARROW LEAVES. THE GREEN BARK WILL SLIP OFF BEST IN SPRING.

1. CUT A ½" THICK WILLOW BRANCH WITH GREEN BARK AND NO JOINTS.

2. MAKE A NOTCH 1-2" FROM THE SLANTED END ON THE LONG SIDE

FRONT SLANT CUT → NOTCH RING BACK ← STRAIGHT CUT

6-12 INCHES

3. CUT THROUGH THE BARK ONLY, IN A RING AROUND THE STICK 1½" BACK FROM THE NOTCH.

4. REMOVE BARK FROM SHADED SECTION. TAP ON THE BARK UNTIL IT LOOSENS, THEN TWIST OFF. DO NOT BREAK.

5. ENLARGE THE NOTCH. KEEP FRONT EDGE STRAIGHT, CUT HALFWAY THROUGH STICK.

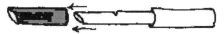

6. REMOVE SHADED AREA TO MAKE THE AIR CHANNEL.

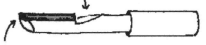

7. REPLACE BARK TUBE AND BLOW!

ACKNOWLEDGEMENTS

This first story in the Dubois Files series has been greatly improved from the input of many people, but most importantly by the following young readers (and their parents) who made suggestions and provided feedback:

William, Ruthy, Clara and Teddy Davis (Minnesota)

Abigale, Julia, and Tessa Ostberg (Arkansas)

Stephanie and Marisa Hoffarth (North Dakota)

Becca Flom (Maryland)

Averie, Niall, and Anders Griffis (Minnesota)

Zack, Kyler and Karlize Barnes (Michigan)

Josiphene Stamper (Michigan)

As always, any final errors are the fault of the author.

Joan H. Young, March 2018

OTHER PUBLISHED WORKS
BY JOAN H. YOUNG

Non-Fiction:
North Country Cache: Adventures on a
National Scenic Trail
North Country Quest: Completing my National
Scenic Trail Adventure
Would You Dare?
Devotions for Hikers

Fiction:
Accidentally Yours
Anastasia Raven Mysteries:
News from Dead Mule Swamp
The Hollow Tree at Dead Mule Swamp
Paddy Plays in Dead Mule Swamp
Bury the Hatchet in Dead Mule Swamp
Dead Mule Swamp Druggist
Dead Mule Swamp Mistletoe

The Dubois Files:
listed at the front of this volume

ABOUT THE AUTHOR

Joan H. Young has enjoyed the out-of-doors her entire life. Highlights of her outdoor adventures include Girl Scouting, which provided yearly training in camp skills, the opportunity to engage in a ten-day canoe trip, and numerous short backpacking excursions. She was selected to attend the 1965 Senior Scout Roundup in Coeur d'Alene, Idaho, an international event to which 10,000 girls were invited. She rode a bicycle from the Pacific to the Atlantic Ocean in 1986, and on August 3, 2010 became the first woman to complete the North Country National Scenic Trail on foot. Her mileage totaled 4395 miles. She often writes and gives media programs about her outdoor experiences.

In 2010 she began writing more fiction, including several award-winning short stories. The Secret Celler is the first book in the Dubois Files mystery series.

Visit booksleavingfootprints.com
for more information.

Made in the USA
Columbia, SC
11 June 2021